The Sea of Tranquillity

FA BR
J
HADDON
M

For Gina Pollinger

— M. H.

For Jake

— C. B.

Text copyright © Mark Haddon 1996
Illustrations copyright © Christian Birmingham 1996

All rights reserved. No part of this publication may be reproduced
or transmitted in any form or by any means, electronic or mechanical,
including photocopy, recording, or any information storage and retrieval system,
without permission in writing from the publisher.

Requests for permission to make copies of any part of the work
should be mailed to: Permissions Department, Harcourt Brace & Company,
6277 Sea Harbor Drive, Orlando, Florida 32887-6777.

First published in Great Britain by HarperCollins Publishers Ltd in 1996

First U.S. edition 1996

Library of Congress Cataloging-in-Publication Data
Haddon, Mark.
The Sea of Tranquillity/by Mark Haddon; illustrated by Christian Birmingham.
p.   cm.
Summary: A man remembers his boyhood fascination with the moon
and the night mankind first bounced through the dust in the Sea of Tranquillity.
ISBN 0-15-201285-0
[1. Moon—Fiction. 2. Space flight to the moon—Fiction.]
I. Birmingham, Christian, ill. II. Title.
PZ7.H1165Se   1996
[Fic]—dc20   95-41267

The text was set in Bembo.

A B C D E

Printed and bound in Italy

MARK HADDON

The Sea of Tranquillity

Illustrated by Christian Birmingham

The Sea of Tranquillity

HARCOURT BRACE & COMPANY

San Diego   New York   London

Years ago
there was a little boy
who had the solar system on his wall.

Late at night he'd lie in bed
with Rabbit
and they would watch the planets
spinning around the sun:
Mars, the tiny space-tomato;
Saturn, sitting in its Frisbee rings;
freezing Pluto, turning slowly in the dark;
Jupiter, Uranus, Neptune, Venus, Mercury,
and Earth.

But of all the weird worlds
that whirled across his bedroom wall,
his favorite was the moon,
a small and bald and ordinary
globe of rock
that loop-the-looped
its way through outer space.

He leaned across the windowsill at night
and watched the moon slide up into the sky
above the biscuit factory.

He borrowed Dad's binoculars
and gazed for hours
at the empty deserts
and the rocky mountains.

It made him dizzy
just to think that he was looking
at another world
two hundred thousand miles away.

He got an atlas of the moon
for Christmas
and he read it
like a storybook.

He dreamed of going there,
of rocketing across the cold, black miles
and landing on the crumbly rock.
He dreamed of visiting
the craters in the atlas:
Prosper Henry, Klaproth, Zach.
He dreamed of driving
in a fat-tired moon mobile,
across the Bay of Rainbows
and the Sea of Rains.

He kept a scrapbook called *The Journey to the Moon*.
Inside were photographs of rockets
taking off from Cape Canaveral
and astronauts in pumped-up suits
and fishbowl helmets
floating in zero gravity
around their little metal rooms.

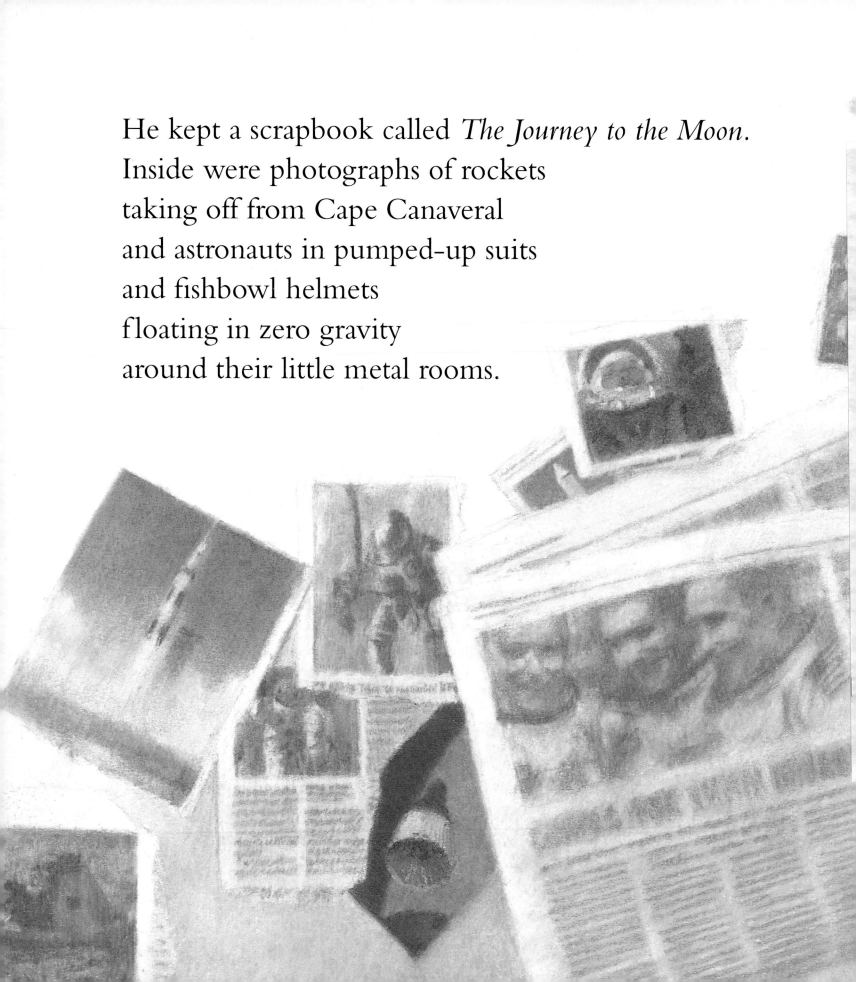

He borrowed library books
and read how astronauts
had orbited the earth
and walked in space
and how they'd flown around the moon itself.
And every night he hoped and hoped
that one day they would find a way to land
and walk across the tiny world
where he had dreamed of walking.

And, eventually, one cloudless night
they did.

Midnight had come and gone,
but the boy was wide awake
and standing at the window
in his dressing gown,
because two astronauts
were walking on the surface of the moon,
two hundred thousand miles
above his bedroom.

At 3:00 A.M.
he went downstairs
and turned the television on.
And there they were,
on the flickery screen,
bouncing slowly through the dust
in the Sea of Tranquillity
like giants in slow motion.

He stayed awake all night
and went to bed at dawn.
The sun was coming up
outside his window
and the moon was fading fast.
He fell asleep
and in his dreams
he walked with them.

That little boy was me.

The solar system wall chart
fell to pieces long ago,
and Rabbit, who is older now,
no longer follows me around
but sits beside my desk
and watches while I work.

Yet still, on cloudless nights,
I sometimes sit beside my bedroom window,
staring at that tiny, distant world.

I think how cold and dark it is up there.
No wind. No clouds. No streams. No sky.
Just rocks and dust.
I think how nothing ever moves,
year after year.

And then I think of those two astronauts,
and how the prints they made
with their big boots
will still be there
tonight,
tomorrow night,
and every night
for millions of years to come.

BOSTON PUBLIC LIBRARY

3 9999 03427 246 6

P

WITHDRAWN
No longer the property of the
Boston Public Library.
Sale of this material benefits the Library.

17

Faneuil Branch Library
419 Faneuil Street
Brighton, MA 02135-1000